the seaside

Translation: Jean Grasso Fitzpatrick

First English language edition published
1986 by Barron's Educational Series, Inc.

© Parramón Ediciones, S.A., 1986

The title of the Spanish edition is *el mar*

All inquiries should be addressed to:
Barron's Educational Series, Inc.
113 Crossways Park Drive
Woodbury, New York 11797
Library of Congress Catalog Card No. 86-5873

International Standard Book No.
Paper: 0-8120-3699-9
Hardcover: 0-8120-5747-3

Library of Congress Cataloging-in-Publication Data

Rius, María.
    Let's discover the seaside.

    (Let's discover series)
    Translation of: *El Mar.*
    Summary: Explains that fishing and tourism are
leading activities in coastal places.
    1. Seashore—Juvenile literature. [1. Seashore.]
I. Parramon, José María. II. Title. III. Series: Let's
discover (Woodbury, N.Y.).
GB451.2.R5813   1986   333.91′7   86-5873
ISBN 0-8120-5747-3
ISBN 0-8120-3699-9 (pbk.)

Printed in Spain
by Gráficas Estella, S.A.
Estella (Navarra)
Register Book Number: 785
Legal Deposit: NA-161-1986

let's discover
the seaside

María Rius
J. M. Parramón

BARRON'S

Woodbury, New York • Toronto

When you look and see water, and more water, and seagulls flying.

When you hear the waves break against the rocks.

When you see fishermen with boats full of fish…

and more fishermen mending
their nets.

When you look at the horizon
and see the boats sailing…

and people traveling on
big ships.

When you see people swimming
in the summertime…

and lying on the sand,
or under umbrellas.

When you look beneath the water and see sand, and rocks like mountains…

and green, waving seaweed and red glowing coral…

big fish and small fish.

And when you see brightly colored sailboats slipping through the waves….

You are at the seaside!

THE SEASIDE

GUIDE FOR PARENTS AND TEACHERS

If you see an intense blue reflection of the calm sea. If you hear a soft murmur that speaks to you of old legends of sirens and sailors. If a strong smell of salt and shellfish comes toward you...pay attention: it is the sea that is speaking to you.

People and the sea

Most of the earth's surface is covered by oceans. Knowing this helps us to understand how important the sea is for people. Since the first settlers arrived on the coasts looking for fish, they recognized the potential of seafaring. People have created a livelihood (commercial fishing), a way of life (in the fishing towns), and a wonderful way of enjoying leisure time (through water sports and the beaches), which the tourists who come to the seaside can share.

Fishing

Fishing has always been very important for seaside towns. Fishing near the coast is called inshore fishing; on the high seas it is called deep-sea fishing. Inshore fisherfolk usually return to port every day with their catch, which is promptly sold. They usually go out in medium-sized boats. The fish, attracted by the bait, are then caught by harpoons, fishing lines with one or more hooks, or they are pulled in with big nets or traps. Deep-sea fisherfolk spend a long time at sea without returning to port. This means that they must have very large boats where the fish can be prepared for sale. Once the fish are caught, they are cleaned, salted, and often frozen. That way the catch is well preserved when it finally arrives back at the port.

Fishing towns

In most towns along the sea coast, the houses are lined up along the shore and painted white to reflect the rays of the sun. This keeps the houses cool inside during the summer. In front of each house there is a wide space where the nets can be spread out and repaired. As it gets late in the day, the sleepy town takes on a different appearance. The fishing boats return to port surrounded by a cloud of seagulls that try to steal fish off the boats. The fish that aren't good enough to eat are thrown back into the water—and are quickly snatched up by the gulls. On the pier, the fish are unloaded and carried to the warehouse. Then the retailers go to the sale and buy the fish they need for their stores. All of this—the return of the boats, the sale, the mending of the nets—is part of an exciting and traditional spectacle that hasn't changed much for hundreds of years.

The beach and water sports

Recently, however, the coastal towns have begun to change. Crowds of tourists looking for the sun and the beaches, and the fun of water sports, have not only made the coastal towns look different, they have often upset the delicate balance of nature in the area. Large apartment buildings have destroyed the beauty of the landscape, while all the pleasure boats have dirtied the beaches. However, along with the changes that aren't very good, the fact remains that people still find in the sea a wonderful place to spend their free time enjoying nature. Whether on the beach or on the water, they have fun with sports such as water skiing, boating (which includes power boats, sailing, or rowing), surfing, or diving.

The sea is an excellent ally. It offers its fish for us to eat, it puts us in contact with other countries and other cultures, it amuses us during our leisure time, and it is an inexhaustible source of inspiration for painters, musicians, and poets.